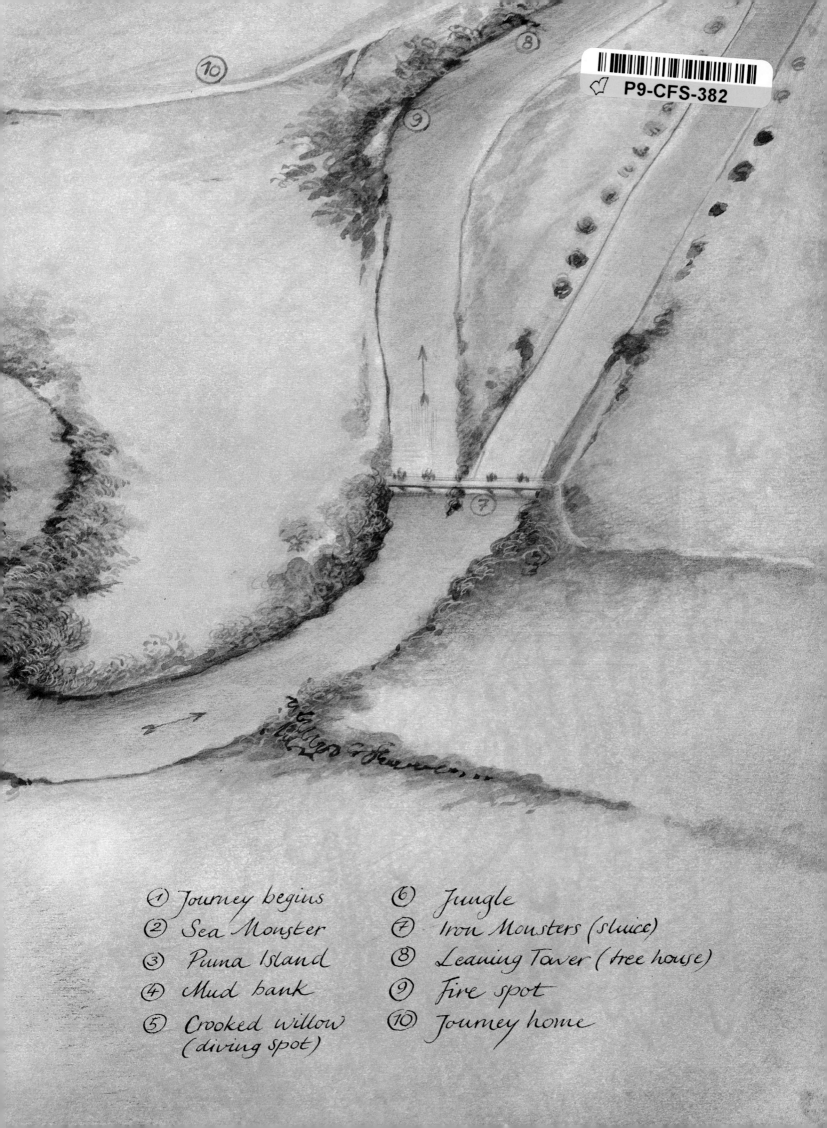

1. Journey begins
2. Sea Monster
3. Puma Island
4. Mud bank
5. Crooked willow (diving spot)
6. Jungle
7. Iron Monsters (sluice)
8. Leaning Tower (tree house)
9. Fire spot
10. Journey home

A Day on the River

by Reinhard Michl

Barron's
Woodbury, New York · Toronto

Paul, Bernie, and Thomas are playing hooky today, and no sooner has the day begun than the three boys are off to the river. Thomas rolls their inner tube ahead of him while Bernie carries the paddles. Besides his fishing rod, Paul has a bag of sandwiches, for the boys will be out on the river all day.

If it were up to the boys, they would spend every day of their lives on the river, and during summer vacations it seems as if they actually live there. No one knows the river better than these three do. When they speak of it, they sound mysterious. No one else in the world knows about the exciting places and things that are just a few bends farther downstream. There, if you knew where to look, you too would find "Puma Island," the "Jungle," and the "Sea Monster."

Shivers run down the boys' spines as they pass by some huge roots and branches that reach up out of the river like claws. Alone, any of the boys would have steered clear of this place. But together they give each other courage.

Sometimes, when they listen to the ominous swirling of the current here, the sunken tree becomes a huge black beast to them, a Sea Monster rising from the mysterious depths of the river.

Puma Island bulges up out of the river like the long, white back of some underwater creature. The high waters leave all sorts of wonderful things washed up on the beaches of the island, and here the boys find the largest and rarest of shells and the most beautiful of stones. Paul even found a snakeskin once. The boys' tree hut in the Leaning Tower is a regular treasure trove by now, filled with the loot they have found on Puma Island.

The banks on the other side of the island are mucky. "Like chocolate pudding," Thomas says. The mud oozes up between his toes, and when he pulls his foot out it makes a loud sucking noise. "How about a mud fight?" he calls to Bernie and Paul. In reply he gets two clumps of juicy mud on his hat. Soon the three boys are covered with mud, with only their teeth gleaming white in their laughing faces.

After the fight they do a lot of swimming and diving from a springy willow branch to rinse off. Then, spluttering and blowing, Thomas surfaces with a piece of bent pipe.

"It's a trumpet," Paul yells.

And Bernie asks, "Where did you find it?"

"There's a funny-looking wild man squatting down there in the roots of the willow. He has all kinds of old stuff. He gave me the trumpet as a present."

"You're full of baloney!" Bernie and Paul say.

"If you don't believe me, go see for yourselves."

They dive, and find that Thomas was right!

(On the poster in the back of this book you can see what it really was that Thomas found in the willow roots.)

Now the boys get into their inner tube again. Softly, their paddles motionless, hardly making a sound, they drift with the current and glide through a tunnel of shimmering green. But soon they emerge from the Jungle, and the Iron Monsters come into view. It's high time for the boys to think about their duties as boatmen again. This stretch of the river calls for skillful seamanship. Because each of the boys often acts as his own captain and helmsman, there can be some confusion at times. But in a real pinch the boys work well together.

The heavy, round heads of the winches hunch down between the broad steel shoulders of the dam like silent, gloomy monsters. The three friends really should stay away from the dam altogether. The yellow signs that say "No Admittance!" are everywhere. But the mechanical monsters hold an irresistible attraction for the boys. They'll just take a quick look. Seen up close, the Iron Monsters aren't nearly so scary.
From the winches with their big interlocking gears, heavy chains hang down into the river. The three friends look longingly at the winches.
"If we could only work them!" says Bernie. But the winches are tightly locked with heavy padlocks. Too bad!

"Look! The river is laughing," Thomas yells. Below them the river is rushing through the dam as if someone had turned on a thousand faucets at once. "The river has a face. You see it? It's laughing and roaring and winking at us."

"Oh, come off it," Paul answers.

Bernie throws a stick into the water. It shoots off like an arrow and soon disappears in the seething foam.

"He just ate it with his big mouth," Paul shouts. "Come on, let's go. I'll get dizzy if I look at this very long."

"And I'm getting hungry," Thomas says.

"We should be putting our treasure away in a safe place too," Bernie urges.

"Right!" Paul agrees. "So let's go to the Leaning Tower and build our campfire!"

Just as they're about to anchor in their harbor near the Leaning Tower, they hear a loud barking from the reeds. Then they see a scruffy little dog coming toward them. The dog may be small, but his bark is so fierce that the boys ready their paddles to fend him off. "Darn! Where did that dog come from?"

Is it possible that…? The same thought occurs to all of the boys at once, and they glance up from the yelping dog to their tree house in the Leaning Tower.

They see a small, dirty foot sticking out of the tree house door. No doubt about it. An intruder has found the boys' secret hiding place and occupied it.

"Moses," a clear, bright voice calls out, "Moses, what's the matter?" Then a head of wild, shaggy blonde hair pops out the door. It belongs to a little girl with a face like a sunflower. She sits there, swinging her dirty feet in the air and petting her little dog. He wags his tail happily and is quiet. "Hi, I'm Eva. You don't have to be afraid of Moses. He's just keeping a good watch on our house. This is where Moses and I live."

It takes a while to get things straight, but before too long Eva understands that the boys are the real owners of the tree house in the Leaning Tower. And the boys realize that Eva does not mean to spend the night here. Actually, she and Moses had moved in just a couple of hours earlier. For two weeks now she has been living in the same apartment building where Bernie, Paul, and Thomas live. Maybe it's because she has such a pretty sunflower face or because her feet are so black with dirt…. At any rate, the three friends suddenly find they are not angry with her at all anymore.

"That's a terrific dog you've got," Bernie says.

The sandwiches are a bit soggy after a long, hot day on the water, but they still taste wonderful once they've been toasted over the fire. Eva knows how to build and tend a fire as well as the boys do, and before they know it they have given her three shells from their treasure trove.

They're all so busy talking, poking the fire, and roasting their sandwiches that no one has noticed how quickly the sun is going down.

"Hey, it's getting dark!" Eva exclaims. "I've got to go home."
"We do, too," Bernie, Paul, and Thomas say.
They carefully put out their fire with a lot of mud.
"We'll take you home," the boys all say at once. To Moses'
delight, Eva gets a place of honor in the inner tube.

After a day on the river, they all fall asleep quickly.
An owl whisks over the water, and the moon climbs up between
the trees. As it shines through our friends' windows, they dream
of new adventures on their river. And Moses growls softly in his
sleep.

THIS PICTURE BOOK doesn't tell an imaginary story. I grew up near the mouth of the Danube, close where the Old Mill stands. I have experienced many days on the river as described here.

Today everything looks totally different. The Old Water (Altwasser) and the old trees are gone, and with them the wild mallards, kingfishers, herons, and many other animals. Children growing up now run on roller skates over a concrete road along a bare, straight dam.

I wanted to relive once more what was once so important and ordinary to my friends and me, with this picture book. This landscape will soon give way to questionable improvements, not only at the Old Mill site, but all along the original flow of the river, with its reed belt and crooked willows. These few miles of "Amazon" in the middle of our landscape will be destroyed by civilization—we simply must preserve this. We cannot sacrifice another mile, not only for the mallard, the kingfisher, and the heron, but for ourselves.

Reinhard Michl

REINHARD MICHL was born in 1948 in Lower Bavaria (West Germany), became a typesetter, and studied graphic arts and later free painting at the Academy of Fine Arts in Munich, where he now lives as an independent creative draftsman.

He illustrated *Jim Knopf*, a book by Michael Ende, and many picture books, including *Findefuchs, Mischa und seine Brüder (Mischa and his Brother)*, and *Das rothaarige Mädchen (The Girl with the Red Hair)*. *A Day on the River* is the first book for which he also wrote the text.

First English language edition published 1985 by Barron's Educational Series, Inc.

Copyright© 1985 K. Thienemanns Verlag, Stuttgart, with respect to original German language edition.

Library of Congress Catalog Card No. 85-18551

International Standard Book No. 0-8120-5715-5

Printed in Germany   56789   987654321

From: A DAY ON THE RIVER by Reinhard Michl, © 1985 by K. Thienemanns Verlag, Stuttgart • Printed in Germany •